THE NEW KID

by Kari James
illustrated by Amanda Haley

MODERN CURRICULUM PRESS
Pearson Learning Group

I just moved to a new neighborhood.
I have to go to a new school. And I
don't have one new friend yet.
I'm afraid.

Everything is new and different here. My teachers are new. All the kids are new.

My new school looks different. It feels different. And it even smells different.

But most of all, I feel different from everyone else.
 I feel lonely. And I don't feel very brave.

My dad says that to make a friend, you have to be a friend. It sounds kind of silly. But I decide to try. What have I got to lose?

I make up my mind to start right away. I won't show that I'm afraid. And I will be as friendly as I can.

After lunch, Ms. Davis says we're having a spelling bee soon. I'm not very good at spelling.
I decide this is it.

I am going to ask Janet to study spelling words with me. Janet sits next to me. She seems pretty nice.

"Hey, Janet," I say. "Do you want to study spelling with me after school? Then we can ride my skateboard."

"Cool," says Janet. "I never rode a skateboard before. Maybe you could teach me."

Yes! I feel better already. I even feel a little brave.

Janet and I practice spelling. We make our own flash cards. Janet helps me with the hard words.

And I teach Janet how to do a jump!
"Wow!" says Janet to me. "You're really brave!"

    I missed the word *reservation*. But I spelled most of the words right.
    And later, Janet and I are going to play ball with a bunch of other kids. Dad was right. I learned to be a friend. So I made a friend. And I don't feel like the new kid anymore.